D1259069

# The Genius Aged 8¼

# JEREMY STRONG

## The Genius Aged 8¼

**Illustrated by Jamie Smith**

Barrington Stoke

First published in 2016 in Great Britain by
Barrington Stoke Ltd
18 Walker Street, Edinburgh, EH3 7LP

www.barringtonstoke.co.uk

Text © 2016 Jeremy Strong
Illustrations © 2016 Jamie Smith

The moral right of Jeremy Strong and Jamie Smith to be
identified as the author and illustrator of this work has been
asserted in accordance with the Copyright, Designs and
Patents Act, 1988

A CIP catalogue record for this book is available
from the British Library upon request

ISBN: 978-1-78112-555-7

Printed in China by Leo

This book is super readable for young readers beginning their
independent reading journey.

*This story is dedicated to everyone at Barrington Stoke. Firstly to congratulate them on winning the IPG Diversity Award and secondly because they let me write very silly stories like this one. I'm sure my teachers at school would never have allowed such things!*

# Contents

# Chapter 1
# What's in a name?

Mrs Poppleton was looking very bulgy around the tummy area.

"Have you been eating too many Jaffa Cakes?" Mr Poppleton asked.

But Mrs Poppleton said no, she hadn't.

"Have you been eating too many chocolate buttons?" Mr Poppleton asked.

But Mrs Poppleton hadn't.

Mr Poppleton stared at his wife's very bulgy tummy.

"You must have eaten SOMETHING," he told her. "Have you swallowed a cow?"

"No."

"An elephant?" he asked.

"NO!"

"How about a tractor? A house? A mountain?" he demanded. "A continent? Africa! Have you eaten Africa?"

"I don't think so," said Mrs Poppleton. "I suppose I could have eaten something in my sleep."

Mr Poppleton's eyes lit up. "Of course! That's it! I bet you ate Africa while you were asleep and didn't notice."

Mrs Poppleton pulled a face. "Oooh! Whatever it is, it just moved. It kicked me."

"Ah!" Mr Poppleton cried. "I know what it is! You must have eaten a footballer."

"Do you really think so?" Mrs Poppleton said. "I don't remember eating a footballer."

"If it kicked you, it must be a footballer," said Mr Poppleton. "Footballers are always kicking. That's their job."

"Well, I suppose you could be right." Mrs Poppleton sighed.

But of course Mr Poppleton wasn't right at all. He was very wrong, because later on that day they found out exactly what was making such a big lump inside Mrs Poppleton's tummy. It was a baby.

The new parents looked at their child.

"He's rather squeaky," Mr Poppleton muttered.

"And squawky," Mrs Poppleton added.

"And his face is very red," said Mr Poppleton.

Then the baby made a rather loud SPLURP!

"Oh my!" said Mr Poppleton. "His bottom has just exploded."

"It does look like it," Mrs Poppleton agreed. "Pass me a clean nappy."

Mr Poppleton looked at Mrs Poppleton. He was horrified. "Don't tell me you've –"

"Don't be daft!" Mrs Poppleton cried, and she turned very red. "The nappy isn't for ME! It's for the BABY!"

"Oh!" Mr Poppleton said with a laugh. "Silly me."

They cleaned up the baby. He gazed back at them. What was he thinking?

Later that day, the midwife called in to see them.

"Have you thought of a name for the baby?" the midwife asked.

"He's called Squeaky Squawker Redface Splurp Bottom," Mrs Poppleton declared, with a proud smile on her face.

"Lovely!" the midwife said. "I do like a nice simple name."

In case you are wondering, the midwife's name was Chubby Chops Nee-Naw-Potato-Nose McDonut. Her friends called her Spud for short.

# Chapter 2
# Who's a genius?

So Mr and Mrs Poppleton's little child was a big surprise to them both, but they were very fond of him. They loved to show him off to the neighbours.

"This is Squeaky Squawker Redface Splurp Bottom," Mrs Poppleton told old Mrs Fudge from next door.

"Ooooh, who's a cutie beauty, my little diddly doodum?" old Mrs Fudge cooed.

Mr and Mrs Poppleton showed
the baby to Mr Boodle, who was their
neighbour on the other side.

"Push me over with a toasted
crumpet!" Mr Boodle cried. "It's a baby!"

Mrs Poppleton thought Mr Boodle
could have made a better comment than
"It's a baby."

"Mrs Fudge thinks he's a cutie
beauty," she hinted.

"Does she now? Well, Mrs Fudge wears glasses for good reason," Mr Boodle grunted.

Mrs Poppleton threw a dark look at Mr Boodle. "I'm going to show my baby to the Mayor now," she said. "I expect SHE will say something NICE."

She took the baby back inside and shut the door.  In fact, she slammed the door to show Mr Boodle just how angry she was with him.  But then she gave her son a big smile.

"You ARE a baby," she told him.  "And you're the best baby in the whole world." She gave her son a smacking wet kiss on each cheek.

"Urgh!" went Squeaky Squawker Redface Splurp Bottom and he shuddered from head to toe in his mother's arms.

Mrs Poppleton was amazed. "Did you hear that, Mr Poppleton?" she cried. "Squeaky spoke! He said 'urgh!' when I kissed him."

"He said 'urgh'?" Mr Poppleton said. "Goodness me, the boy's a genius. He's only a week old."

"He IS a genius," Mrs Poppleton agreed. "One day he could be Prime Minister. One day he could win the Nobel Prize for Physics. One day he could ..."

But, in the meantime, what Squeaky Squawker did each day was grow.  He grew very fast indeed.

One sunny afternoon the happy family was out in the garden playing Toss The Baby Over The Pond.

This was their favourite game.

Mrs Poppleton would stand on one side of the pond and Mr Poppleton would stand on the other.  Then they would throw the baby to each other.  Of course,

sometimes they missed catching him
and the baby would land in the pond.
Then they would laugh and fish him out
and say things like, "Who's a wet baby!"

Then, on that one sunny afternoon, a dripping Squeaky looked up at his mother as she fished him out of the pond and he said, "Stop it, Mummy!"

Mrs Poppleton almost fell into the pond herself. "Mr Poppleton, did you hear that?" she said. "Squeaky said 'Mummy'! He really did!"

Mr Poppleton hurried over. He beamed at the baby and Squeaky looked up at his father and he said, "Daddy, stop dropping me in the pond!"

"Did you hear that?" Mr Poppleton cried. "He called me Daddy!"

The two parents danced round their son singing and shouting at him. "Mummy! Daddy! Daddy! Mummy!" In their excitement, they both had to be very careful not to trip over each other and into the pond.

Squeaky gurgled and said "Mummy" and "Daddy" again and again until Mr Poppleton took his son from his wife and held him in his arms.

"You are SO clever, Squeaky Squawker Redface Splurp Bottom!" he said.

The baby shook his head, hard. "Alfred!" he said. "Alfred!"

"What's Squeaky Squawker Redface Splurp Bottom saying now?" Mrs Poppleton asked.

And the baby shook his head even more. "Alfred! Not that silly Squeaky Squawker stuff. Call me Alfred, or even Alfie, if you must!"

"I think he wants to be called Alfie," Mrs Poppleton said.

"He does indeed," Mr Poppleton agreed with pride. "Fancy that. He's so young and he knows just what he wants. The boy's a genius."

So from then on they called their son Alfie, which was a VERY GOOD THING because, you see, Alfie thought that being called Squeaky Squawker Redface Splurp Bottom was just about the most ridiculous thing EVER. And he was quite right too. Alfie was a much more sensible name.

## Chapter 3
## Too many teeth and too little exercise

Months passed. Years passed. And very soon it was time for Alfie to go to school. Alfie liked learning and he learned lots at school.

The school that Alfie went to was called the Mostly Mish-Mash Banana Brain Academy.

It was quite small. It only had three classes.

Class 1 was for anyone who was 4, 6, 8 or 10 years old.

Class 2 was for children who were 5, 7, 9 or 11 years old.

Class 3 was for anyone older than 11. But there weren't any children older than 11, so Class 3 was completely empty.

Miss Crumbwarble was the Head Teacher. She was about 100 years old and had false teeth which kept falling out.

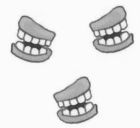

She kept several spare sets of teeth in her handbag. Her fingers were always covered in bruises and little plasters. This was because whenever she looked in her handbag for a strawberry and pickle sandwich, or a hamster, at least one pair of spare teeth would snap at her. She would go "OW!" and pull out her hand with a pair of false teeth gripping a finger. Once she pulled out THREE pairs of false teeth at one go!

One day a school inspector came to check the school. He was also about 100 years old and he was called Mr Grrrr. He scowled at everything, even nice harmless things like door knobs and potted plants. But what he didn't scowl at was Miss Crumbwarble. He seemed to like her.

However, Mr Grrrr found lots of things wrong at the Mostly Mish-Mash Banana Brain Academy.

"Some of your lessons are too long," he told the teachers and the Head Teacher.

"Oh dear," they sighed.

"And some of your lessons are too short," Mr Grrrr added.

Miss Crumbwarble's face lit up. She'd had a genius idea. "Why don't we take some bits off the lessons that are too long and add them to the lessons that are too short?" she said. "Then all the lessons should be about the right length."

"That's an excellent idea," Mr Grrrr told Miss Crumbwarble and he beamed a smile at her.

"However, there is another big problem," Mr Grrrr said. "Your children don't get enough exercise. They should be doing lots of jumping, catching, skipping and sneezing. Sneezing is good for the nose. I shall come back in a week to check."

Then Mr Grrrr went away, but not before he had given Miss Crumbwarble his home address and telephone number and email address and told her exactly which bus to catch to his house.

Well, Miss Crumbwarble came up with a terrific plan.  She gave every child in the school a bike, except for the youngest ones.  She gave them scooters.

"Now then," Miss Crumbwarble said. "You must cycle round all day and do your school work while you're cycling! Work and exercise at the same time!  I think you will all LOVE my clever idea!"

Sadly, as soon as the children started pedalling AND trying to work at the same time they couldn't see where they were going. They kept crashing into each other and falling over.

One day there was such a big crash that six ambulances had to come to the school. The fire brigade came with two fire engines and special tools to free the children from the tangle of bicycles. The police came to see whose fault the crash was and they decided everyone was to blame. They arrested everyone except Alfie, who hadn't gone on his bike at all because he thought it was a stupid idea in the first place.

"Oh dear," Miss Crumbwarble wailed. "Mr Grrrr is coming tomorrow and we are in SUCH a mess! What are we going to do?"

Alfie knew exactly what to do.

"It's difficult for the teachers to teach a class full of 4, 6, 8 and 10 year olds at the same time," he said. "You should put the 4 to 6 year olds in Class 1, the 7 to 9 year olds in Class 2 and the 9 to 11 year olds in Class 3.  That will make it easier for the teachers to teach and it will save time.  Then you can use the saved time to have PE lessons and that way the children will get their exercise."

Miss Crumbwarble and the teachers stared at Alfie in amazement.  "The boy's a genius!" they chorused.

The next day Mr Grrrr turned up and he was astonished to see the changes at the school. He wanted to know how it had happened.

"It was Alfie's idea," Miss Crumbwarble said with pride.

"Well, scrub my onions!" Mr Grrrr declared. "The boy's a genius. I'm going to make him Head Teacher right away."

So Alfie became the Head Teacher of the school and Miss Crumbwarble didn't have a job any more.

Luckily this didn't matter because Mr Grrrr asked her to marry him. (In fact, that might have been part of Mr Grrrr's plan when he made Alfie the Head Teacher.)

The teachers at the school gave Miss Crumbwarble a special wedding present of teeth-proof gloves that she could wear whenever she had to rummage about in her handbag.

# Chapter 4
# One way? No way?
# It's all the wrong way!

Time went by and soon Alfie Poppleton was 7 years old and he was very busy at school.

Not only was he the Head Teacher, but he was also still a pupil. Sometimes he even had to teach himself.

Alfie and his parents lived a mile from the school, so Alfie always went to school on his bike. One afternoon he left school to go home for his tea. He hadn't gone very far when he came to a road with a new sign on it that said NO ENTRY.

Alfie looked around for another way home. He went a little way and soon he came to another road with a NO ENTRY sign on it. He hunted about and found a third road with a NO ENTRY sign on it.

Alfie couldn't get home. Every way he tried he ended up at a road with a NO ENTRY sign. All the streets were one-way streets, but they all went the same way. Bikes and cars and buses

and trucks couldn't go DOWN the road, but they could come UP the road. Alfie decided he would just have to go down a road with a NO ENTRY sign or he would never be able to get home.

And so Alfie set off, but half way down the road he met a police car coming UP the road. The car stopped and a policeman got out.

"You're going the wrong way down a one-way street," the policeman said. "I shall have to arrest you and take you to the police station."

So the policeman arrested Alfie and they drove up the road to the end.  The policeman began to drive around looking for a way back to the police station, but all the roads said NO ENTRY on them.

"Bother," the policeman said.  "I shall have to go the wrong way down the street or I shall never get back to the police station."

But of course half way down the road the police car met another police car coming up the other way.  The two cars stopped.

"You're going the wrong way along this street," the second policeman said to the first policeman.  "I shall have to arrest you."

So now there were two policemen and Alfie in the second police car. They got to the top of the road and tried to get back the way they needed to go, but all the roads said NO ENTRY. So the second policeman drove the wrong way down the road and they met a third police car. The third policeman arrested the first two, and Alfie.

This went on until there were 15 arrested police officers and Alfie all squashed into one police car.

At last they got to the police station.

The sergeant in charge was very angry. "This is ridiculous!" she said. "The new one-way system that the Mayor has told us to put in place doesn't work at all. Cars can only go one way because all the one-way streets point the same way. It's crazy."

Then all the police officers started arguing with each other, so Alfie crept away and went across to the Town Hall to speak to the Mayor.

"Your new one-way system is a disaster," Alfie told the Mayor. "The cars can only go one way. If you have a one-way system you must make sure one half of the roads go one way and the other half of the roads go the other way. Then everyone will be able to get to where they want to go."

The Mayor stared at Alfie in amazement.

"Goodness me, what a brilliant idea," she said. "The boy's a genius! You'll make a much better job of being the Mayor than me. Here you are, wear this!"

And the Mayor handed over the special gold chain that she wore around her neck to show how important she was. She put the chain over Alfie's shoulders.

"There! Now you are Mayor
of Underpants," she told him.
"Congratulations!"

The town was called Underpants
because when the Queen came along
to name the town a big wind blew Mr
Grrrr's pants off his washing line. They
landed on the Queen's head just as she
said, "I name this town – SPLAT! – Ooh!
Underpants!"

# Chapter 5
# It's war!

Poor Alfie.  Now he had twice as much work as before.  Not only was he the Head Teacher of the school, he was also the Mayor and he was still only 7 and 3/4 years old.  But Alfie's biggest challenge was about to come.

There was an awfully big row going on.  It was on the news everywhere – in the papers and on TV.  Alfie and his mother and father were watching as the Prime Minister spoke to the nation.

"Our great country has never faced such a threat," the Prime Minister said. "We must stand up for what is right! Yes, we will fight!  We shall fight them

on the beaches!  We shall fight them up the trees and in Mrs Binkybonk's Café! I have ordered the army to prepare for war!"

"IT'S WAR!" the newspapers and the TV screamed.

'Oh dear,' Alfie thought.  'This isn't good at all.'

"No it isn't," said Mr Poppleton, and Mrs Poppleton agreed.

In fact, most of the country agreed, especially Mrs Binkybonk.  It wasn't good at all.  But what was this war all about?

CHEESE!

The British Prime Minister had been to lunch with the French President.  It was a very long and very fancy lunch, and when they got to the cheese course at the end the French President said that France made the best cheese in the world.

The British Prime Minister agreed that French cheese was very fine, but then she said that the British not only make the best cheese in the world, but they in fact invented cheese.

"YOU INVENTED CHEESE?" the French President spluttered. "*Non, non, non!* We, the French, invented cheese."

"The FRENCH? Don't be ridiculous," the British Prime Minister roared. "Your cheeses stink like prehistoric socks worn by dinosaurs and they taste even worse!"

"Socks! Cheese! Never!" the French President said. Then he told his army, "This means war!"

"This means war," the British Prime Minister told HER army.

"PREPARE FOR BATTLE!" the leaders each told their countries.

Alfie listened to this and heaved a big sigh. As if he didn't have enough to do already.

But he knew straight away what the answer was, of course.

Alfie wrote a letter to the French President and the British Prime Minister inviting them both to dinner.

When the two leaders arrived they glared at each other and at Alfie too. Alfie ignored the glares.

"Now then," Alfie said. "Nobody wants war. The two of you will have to talk it out between you and agree on a peaceful answer. So, you sit at that end of the table and you sit there."

"Is there dinner?" the French President said. He was very hungry and a little bit puzzled. "What are we going to eat?"

"Cheese," Alfie said. "This dinner is a cheese course only. You have 20 different cheeses to eat. You must tell me which are British and which are French. You must also tell me which ones you like best."

"This is very silly," the two leaders muttered.  They were still glaring at each other and at Alfie.

"No," Alfie said, and his voice was very stern.  "It's not silly at all.  Going to war is very silly.  Now, eat your cheeses."

So they did. The French President decided which cheeses were French and made them his favourites. And the British Prime Minister chose 10 cheeses that she thought were British and made them HER favourites.

Alfie checked the results. He smiled. Half the cheeses the French President thought were French were in fact British. And half the cheeses the British Prime Minister thought were British were French.

"My results show that you are evenly matched," Alfie said. "In fact, you are both right, and you're both wrong. Both countries make great cheeses. I also discovered that countries all over the world make cheese. The idea of cheese was invented by lots of people in lots of different places at round about the same time. So, there's nothing to fight over, is there?"

The two leaders looked at each other. They weren't glaring any more.

"The boy's a genius!" they chorused. "We don't have to go to war at all!"

The people of Britain and the people of France were delighted. No one had wanted to go to war in the first place.

"Alfie Poppleton is a genius!" they said and they made Alfie the Prime Minister of Britain AND the President of France.

Now Alfie really did have a lot to do.

He was

- The Head Teacher of the Mish-Mash Banana Brain Academy

- The Mayor of Underpants

- The Prime Minister of Britain

AND

- The President of France ...


- Plus he had to go to school as a pupil because he still had plenty of learning to do.


All this was quite an achievement for someone who started life called Squeaky Squawker Redface Splurp Bottom.  And who was still only 8 and a 1/4.